A Child's First
PICTURE DICTIONARY

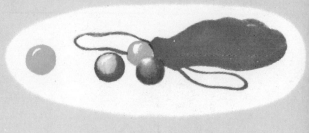

This is my book

Tammy Camacho

What This Book Can Do For Your Child

Give your child the <u>right</u> start in learning to read. This book has been prepared for just that purpose by Mrs. Lilian Moore, Specialist in Reading.

The words have been carefully selected. The child's own world—his home, his family, his play-life—has been woven into the presentation of the key words. This enjoyment of the familiar will at the same time contribute to the child's success in reading when he goes to school.

<u>If your child is ready to read</u>—<u>if he has begun to receive reading instruction</u>—this book will be most useful to him, because the 302 key words in it appear with great frequency in first- and second-grade readers.

As a parent, you know that your child learns most readily when his interest is aroused; that he learns most easily about the things with which he has some experience; that he learns most naturally through interesting repetition. You will find that the author has faithfully adhered to these basic principles in her fresh and lively text.

A Child's First PICTURE DICTIONARY

By LILIAN MOORE

Illustrations by
Nettie Weber *and* Charles Clement

WONDER BOOKS • NEW YORK
A Division of Grosset & Dunlap, Inc.
A National General Company

For DICK MOORE

Library of Congress Catalog Card Number: 67-20678

ISBN: 0-448-01600-1 (Wonder Paperback Edition)
ISBN: 0-448-02248-6 (Trade Edition)
ISBN: 0-448-03668-1 (Library Edition)

1972 PRINTING

across

Green light!
The children go
across the street.

animal

The dog is
an **animal.**

The horse is an **animal.**

after

The cat runs **after** a ball.
Baby runs **after** the kitten.

apple

Apples grow
on **apple** trees.

airplane

The **airplane** is coming
down from the sky.

around

Around and around
goes the merry-go-round.

airport

This is the **airport.**
The airplane will land at this
airport.

ate

Joey was hungry. He **ate**
until he could eat no more.

b B
baby

Mother is teaching
the **baby** to walk.

ball

Beach **ball**

Snow**ball**

It's fun to play with any **ball.**

balloon

Big balloons!
Little balloons!
Who wants to buy
a **balloon?**

barn

Into the **barn** goes the hay.

bear

This baby **bear** lives in the
zoo with Mother **Bear.**

bed

Jane puts her doll to **bed.**

bicycle

Watch Billy
on his **bicycle!**

big

Sue is little.
Mother is **big.**

Sue's apron is little.
Mother's is **big.**

birthday

Today is Jo's **birthday.**
Happy **birthday!**

black

These pieces of coal are
black.

My shoes are **black.**

blow

Betty likes to **blow**
soap bubbles.

boat

The boys sail their
boats in the park.
The little **boat** is winning!

book

Mother reads to Baby
from his **book.**

box

This **box** has
a surprise in it. Look!

boy

Tim is a lucky
boy. He got
a football
for his birthday.

bread

Jelly on **bread!**
Mm-m-m. Good!

b B

brown

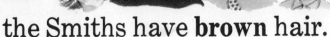

All
the Smiths have **brown** hair.

build

What will Bobby **build**
with his blocks?

building

He's making
a tall **building.**

bus

All aboard the school **bus!**

c C

cake

Chocolate **cake** tonight!

calf

The baby **calf** stays close
to Mother Cow.

call

My dog comes
when I **call** him.

candy

Peppermints,
lollipops —
Which **candy** shall
I choose?

car

Father drives to work in a big blue **car.**

children

The Wilsons have four **children** — two boys and two girls.

cat

This is Judy's **cat.** She calls him Toby.

Christmas

It's **Christmas** morning.

Merry **Christmas!**

catch

Peter has to run fast to **catch** this ball!

circus

Clowns, elephants, acrobats — all in the **circus.**

chair

This is Father's favorite **chair.**

city

Tall buildings — streets — cars — many people. This is the **city!**

c C

climb

Poor kitten!
Father has to **climb**
a ladder to get her.

clown

This is Toto,
the circus **clown.**

coat

Mother is buying a new
winter **coat**
for Peggy.

cold

What a **cold** winter
day! It is so **cold** you can
see your breath!

cook

Mother is going
to **cook**
supper.
Debby loves to help.

country

Trees and
fields, cows and
chickens – it's
the **country!**

cow

Bossie
is the best **cow**
on the farm.

cry

Baby is so unhappy.
Hear him **cry!**

dance

Mother
plays and we **dance.**

day

Good morning!
Davy's **day** begins.
Good night!
Davy's **day** ends.

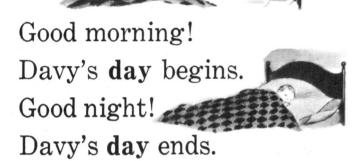

deep

Father swims in **deep** water.
It's way over his head.

dinner

The Dobbs family
always eats **dinner** together.

dog

This **dog**
can do tricks.

doll

This is the **doll**
Janey wants.
It can say "Mama."

door

This is the **door**
to Dickie's room.

down

Down the slide
goes Pat.
Up he climbs,
then —
down he goes again!

d D

drink

It is so good to get a **drink** when you are thirsty!

drive

My dad can **drive** a truck.

drum

Boom! Boom! Jim has a new **drum.**

duck

This **duck** likes his pond.

e E

egg

A hen just laid this **egg.**

elephant

This **elephant** lives in the zoo. See! He can pick up a tiny peanut.

engine

The **engine** pulls all the other cars.

engineer

The **engineer** has charge of the engine.

fall

Careful, Johnny,
or you will **fall!**

family

This will be
a picture of
our whole **family.**

far

Far, far away
I see an airplane.
It looks very small.

farm

This is a **farm.**
Food comes from farms.

fast

A bicycle goes **fast.**
A train goes faster.

fat

What a **fat,**
roly-poly puppy!

feed

Baby cannot
eat by herself.

Mother must **feed** her.

find

Frank is looking
for his ball.
He can't **find** it.
Can you **find** it
for him?

f F

fire

Fire!
The building's on **fire**!

fireman

The firemen
will put out the fire.

One **fireman** is
bringing the hose.

first

Jackie is **first**
in line.

fish

Rudy likes to watch the **fish**
swimming in the bowl.

five

Five fingers on my hand.
Five toes on my foot.

fix

Everyone brings things
for Dad to **fix.**

flag

The **flag** is flying
from the pole.

fly

Roy has just made
a model plane.

Watch it **fly!**

food

This good **food** keeps us well.

friend

Joyce is Judy's best **friend.**

found

See what puppy has **found.**
The slipper that Paul lost!

four

A horse has **four** legs.
A car has **four** wheels.

fruit

An apple is a **fruit.**
A banana is a **fruit.**
These are fruits, too.

fox

The farmer is hunting for this **fox.** It steals his hens.

fun

It's **fun** to play in the snow!

funny

Look at our **funny** snow man!

g G

game

Tag is Jimmie's favorite **game.**

garden

Sally has a flower **garden** in her own back yard.

gate

Ed is swinging on the **gate.**

girl

Julie is the little **girl.**
The big **girl** is Kate.

go

Green light!
The cars and people **go.**

goat

Billy, the **goat,** has whiskers on his chin!

gold

Father has a **gold** watch.

Mother has a **gold** ring.

good

Food tastes **good** when you are hungry.

Bed feels **good** when you are sleepy.

What else is **good?**

grandfather

Martin Jones says,

"This is **Grandfather** Jones.

He is my dad's father.

This is **Grandfather** Brown.

He is Mother's father."

grandmother

"This is **Grandmother** Jones.

She is Dad's mother.

This is **Grandmother** Brown.

She's Mother's mother."

grass

Father cuts
the long
green **grass.**

grocer

Mr. Hill is a **grocer.** He sells
groceries.

grocery

This is Mr. Hill's **grocery** store.

ground

Patty planted a seed in the
ground. She watered it.

grow

Then Patty watched the seed
grow and **grow.**

guess

"Can you **guess**
who this is?"

h H

hand

In which **hand**
is the penny?

happy

Baby is **happy**
with her new toy.

hat

Oh!
Look at Mother's new **hat!**

hatch

Mother Hen will sit on this
egg. Then it will **hatch.**
Out will come a baby chick!

help

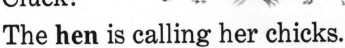

Ben has found a good
way to **help** his mother.

hen

Cluck!
The **hen** is calling her chicks.

hide

We are playing
hide-and-seek.

Rob has found
a place to **hide.**

high

There goes my balloon —
too **high** to catch now!

hill

Down the **hill.** Fun!
Up the **hill.** Work!

hit

Andy is ready
to **hit** the ball.

hold

This is all
Daddy can **hold.**

home

Good! Aunt Sara
is at **home** today.

horse

Peter rides
his **horse.**

hot

This cocoa is too **hot** to drink.

Now it is
just right!

house

A new **house** is being built.

hungry

Here comes food,
hungry birds!

i I

ice cream

What a big **ice-cream** cone!

in

Nicky's toys are **in** this box.

inside

It's raining.

We must play **inside** today.

into

The boys have fun jumping **into** the water.

j J

jack-in-the-box

Up he pops when you open the box.

jack-o'-lantern

Tony made this one out of a big pumpkin for Hallowe'en.

juice

Squeeze the oranges! We like orange **juice** for breakfast.

jump

It is Connie's turn to **jump.**

k K
kind
Johnny is **kind** to his pet.

l L
lamb
A **lamb** is a baby sheep.

kitchen
Mother cooks our meals in the **kitchen.**

large
Here is a **large** package.

Here is a small package.

kite
The **kite** goes sailing up in the wind.

last
Mary is **last** in line.

kitten

Mother Cat is watching her **kitten** play.

laugh
The clown is so funny that the children **laugh.**

l L

letter

Here's a **letter**
for you, Dick!

light

It's getting dark.
Turn on the **light!**

like

Baby hugs her
toy bear. "I **like** you, Teddy
Bear," she says.

lion

You can see
a **lion** in
the zoo.

live

We **live**
here – Mother,
Daddy, and
I.

long

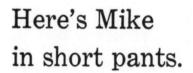

Here's Mike in **long** pants.

Here's Mike
in short pants.

look

Look, Scottie!
Who is it?

lost

Jackie has
lost something.
Do you see it?

make

We like to **make** things out of clay.

man

Father is a **man**.

Some day I will be a **man**, too.

many

One family lives here.

Many families live in this house.

march

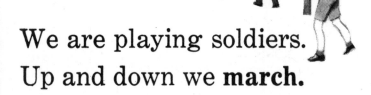

We are playing soldiers. Up and down we **march**.

may

Mother says, "You **may** go out now."

meat

The butcher sells us **meat**.

meow

"**Meow, meow**," says the hungry cat.

milk

This **milk** is for us.

milkman

The **milkman** brings our milk every morning.

m M

monkey

See the little **monkey** dance.

He wants a penny.

more

The big trunk holds **more** than the little one.

morning

Good **morning.**
How bright the sun is!
It's time to get up.

Mother

Al gives **Mother** something he made.

mouse

The **mouse** comes out of his hole.

Sniff! Sniff!
He smells cheese.

mouth

Our dog carries the newspaper all the way home in his **mouth.**

near

We live **near** our school. We don't have far to walk.

night

It's dark.
Night is here.
It's bedtime.

nest

The bluebirds are building a **nest.** It will be their home.

nine

Nine boys make a base-ball team.

new

New shoes for Nancy!

noon

It's **noon.**
Time for lunch!

nickel

A **nickel** will buy as much as five pennies will.

nose

I feel a sneeze in my **nose!**

o O

off

Ben is learning to ride
his bike. Oh! Oh! he fell **off.**

old

Tom's overalls
are too **old** to mend.

on

Ben can stay
on his bike now.

He can ride!

one

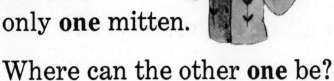

Oh! I have
only **one** mitten.

Where can the other **one** be?

open

The window
is **open.**

orange

An **orange** is a fruit —
good to eat.
Oranges grow on trees,
where it is warm.

out

My tooth
just came **out!**

over

There goes the ball,
over the fence!

Toby goes under
the fence to get it.

pail

Peg fills a **pail** with sand.

paint

Chris likes to **paint** pictures.

pair

A **pair** of gloves.
A **pair** of shoes.

Two things alike make a **pair.**

paper

Father makes **paper** hats for Freddie.

park

Grass, trees, and space to play. We like the **park.**

parrot

This bird is a **parrot.** He can say some words.

party

This is Mollie's **party.**

paste

Freddie's paper hat is torn. Father will mend it with **paste.**

p P

paw

The boy
is taking a
splinter out of the dog's **paw**.

peanuts

Hot roasted
peanuts!

pen

Daddy fills
his fountain **pen**
with ink.

pencil

Jane has a new **pencil** box.

penny

May found a new **penny**.

people

The bus is full of **people**.

pet

Charlie likes
the **pet** shop.

picnic

Everything tastes good
at a **picnic**.

pig

This little **pig**
loves to roll in the mud!

pigeon

Judy feeds the pigeons
in the park.

One **pigeon**
knows Judy!

plant

This **plant** is
green and healthy.

This **plant** needs
sunshine and wàter.

play

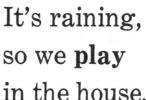

It's raining,
so we **play**
in the house.

playground

The sun's out.

Off we go
to the **playground**!

please

"Help me, **please**!"

pocket

See what was
in Paul's **pocket**!

policeman

This **policeman** directs
traffic on the corner.

p P

postman

Here's the **postman**!
Any letters for us?

present

"A **present** for you, Mother!"

pretty

How **pretty** Ellen is
in her Easter clothes!

prize

Brownie won
a **prize**
in the pet show. The **prize**
was a blue ribbon.

pull

Pull hard
so our side will win!

puppy

Which **puppy** would
you choose for a pet?

push

It is hard
to **push** this heavy cart.

puzzle

Ann has a new picture **puzzle**
She is trying to put the pieces
together.

q Q

quick

Here's Rover!

Quick, quick, rabbit.

Into your hole!

quiet

Sh! Be **quiet.**

Father's asleep.

r R

rabbit

The little **rabbit** is safe in his burrow.

race

Who swims the faster?

Who's going to win this **race?**

radio

Randy has his own little **radio.**

rain

The **rain** comes down.
The umbrellas go up.

ran

Joan **ran** to meet her daddy.

read

"Please **read** to me!"

r R

red

Red cherries.
A **red** Valentine.
Whose **red** hat?

ride

Jim gives
his little brother a **ride.**

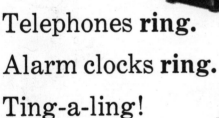

ring

Telephones **ring.**
Alarm clocks **ring.**
Ting-a-ling!

river

Fast boats,
slow boats — all
kinds of boats sail
down the **river.**

roll

Eddie can **roll**
his hoop way
down the street.

room

Lou and his brother
sleep in the same **room.**

rooster

"Cock-a-doodle-do!"
crows the **rooster,**
early in the morning.

round

A ball is **round.**
Marbles are **round.**
What else is **round?**

same

Our hats
are the **same.**

Our coats are different.

sand

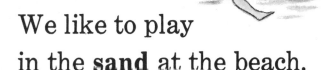

We like to play
in the **sand** at the beach.

Santa Claus

Toys for Christmas!

saw

Bert is using Father's sharp
saw to cut the board.

school

Wags followed Frank
into the **school** building.

scissors

See what Sara cut out
with a pair of **scissors!**

scooter

Down the street
goes Mike on his **scooter!**

sea

It's fun
to watch
the ships at **sea.**

s S

see

Tim can **see**
Beth. His eyes are open.

Beth cannot **see** Tim.

set

Bill **set** the box
down on the chair.

seven

The **seven**
hats are for
Lily's party.

shake

Bert's dog
can **shake** hands.

shoes

Jeff likes his shiny
brown **shoes.** He
polished them himself.

short

This ladder is too
short to reach the roof.

show

We saw a
funny puppet **show** in school.

shut

Please **shut** the
window! The rain
is coming in.

sing

We **sing** in school.

sister

This is Don
and his little **sister,** Ruth.

sit

See Katy's dolls **sit** up.

six

"A half-dozen eggs, please."

"Here you are—**six** eggs."

Six makes a half-dozen.

skip

Walking
is too slow!

Judy likes to **skip.**

sky

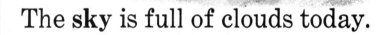

The **sky** is full of clouds today.

sled

The snow
is clean and hard,
just right for a ride on a **sled.**

sleep

Mother is singing,
"Sleep, my little one, **sleep."**

s S

slide

Watch out!
Jack wants
to **slide** down.

small

Jonathan wears a **small** hat.
Daddy wears a large hat.
They can't wear each other's
hats!

snow

So much **snow** to shovel!

soft

How **soft** a bunny's fur is!

spring

Buds on the trees,
flowers growing—
It is **spring**!

squirrel

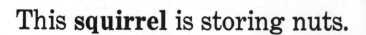

This **squirrel** is storing nuts.

stand

No seats
left! We **stand.**

star

"**Star** light!
Star bright!
First **star** I see tonight…"

step

When I walk
with Daddy I have
to take a long **step.**

stick

See Rex carry the **stick!**

stone

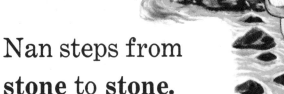

Nan steps from
stone to **stone.**

stop

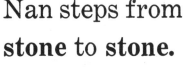

A whistle
blows.
Cars **stop.**
People **stop.**

store

The girls make believe
they are buying groceries
at Johnny's **store.**

street

We live on this **street.**

string

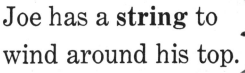

Joe has a **string** to
wind around his top.

suit

Dan has a new **suit.**

s S

supper

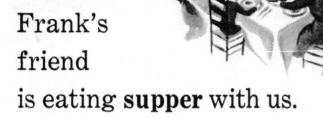

Frank's friend is eating **supper** with us.

surprise

Here' a **surprise** for Susan!

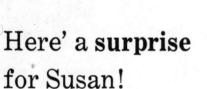

swim

Sam can see the fish **swim.**

swing

"How do you like to go up in a **swing?**"

t T

tall

No, Pete, you aren't **tall** enough!

telephone

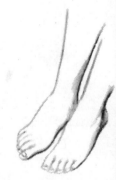

Baby wants to answer the **telephone.**

ten

You have **ten** fingers and **ten** toes.

three

A tricycle has **three** wheels.

top

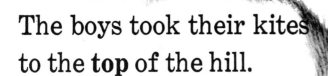

The boys took their kites to the **top** of the hill.

toy

Baby likes one **toy** best.

track

Here is the station. The train will come in on this **track.**

train

Here comes the **train** now.

truck

An oil **truck.**

A coal **truck.**

Trucks carry many things.

turkey

This **turkey** lives on a big farm.

turtle

Carl has a pet **turtle.**

two

Two flowers on this stem,

two wheels on a bike,

two eyes in your head!

u U

umbrella

What a big **umbrella!**

under

Oh, but see
who is **under** it.

up

Look **up** at the sky!

upstairs

"Good night!"

Johnny is going
upstairs to bed.

v V

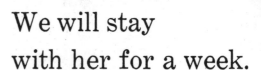

vegetable

We have a **vegetable** garden.

visit

We are off for a
visit to Grandma.

We will stay
with her for a week.

w W

wagon

Jake made this **wagon.**

wake

Wake up!

walk

Lucy likes
to **walk**
on Main Street.

wall

Dad hangs a
picture on the **wall.**

wash

Ruth has to **wash**
her doll's clothes.

water

The street
cleaner opens
the hydrant.

The **water**
rushes out.

wheel

This is a **wheel.** Many things
move on wheels.

whistle

Jerry blows
his **whistle** loudly.

white

A polar bear
is **white.**

wind

How the **wind**
blows!

It makes
the clothes dance.

w W

winter

Sleds and snow—
red cheeks, cold feet—
It's **winter!**

work

We all **work.**

x X

xylophone

Hard to say,
easy to play.

y Y

yard

Peter has a tent
in his **yard.**

young

Baby is **young.**
Grandma
is old.

z Z

zebra

You can tell
a **zebra** by his stripes.

zipper

Zip down to open!
Zip up to close!

zoo

Come see us
at the **zoo!**